D1053291

REALLY STUPID STORIES FOR REALLY SMART ★ KIDS ★

Running Press Kids
Hachette Book Group
1290 Avenue of the Americas, New York, NY 10104
www.runningpress.com/rpkids
@RP_Kids

Printed in the United States of America

First Edition: October 2020

Published by Running Press Kids, an imprint of Perseus Books, LLC, a subsidiary of Hachette Book Group, Inc. The Running Press Kids name and logo is a trademark of the Hachette Book Group.

Print book cover and interior design by Marissa Raybuck

Library of Congress Control Number: 2019954907

ISBNs: 978-0-7624-9623-5 (hardcover),
978-0-7624-9622-8 (ebook)

LSC-C

10 9 8 7 6 5 4 3 2 1

REALLY STUPID STORIES ★★★★ FOR ★★★★ REALLY SMART KIDS

by **ALAN KATZ**
Illustrated by **GARY BOLLER**

RP|KIDS
PHILADELPHIA

TABLE OF CONTENTS

THE STUPID MESSAGE AT THE BEGINNING OF THE BOOK

It's a good thing you're reading this book.

Because if you *don't* read this book all the way through to the end, your head might fall off.

Which is exactly what happened to Vincent Newman.

Vincent said, "No way. I'm not gonna read that book," and then . . .

PLOP!

His head fell off and rolled into a field, where some dogs played soccer with it.

The final score was Bulldogs 7, Mutts 5.

Close game.

Too bad Vincent didn't really get to see it.

When Jessica Phillips ignored this book, her ears turned into antlers.

It was all pretty shocking, especially when her family started hanging their coats on Jessica.

Miss Joy, one of the best librarians anywhere, recommended this book to Danny Valenti.

But he turned it down.

Within minutes, his rear end grew to the size of an elephant's—which made it very hard for him to lie on his bed without his trunk hitting the ceiling.

(Oh yes, he had also grown a trunk.)

Rachel Brown *thought about* reading this book, but she decided she didn't like its cover. Now that Rachel's arms are 17 feet long, she

realizes that it's true—you can't tell a book by its cover.

Jordan Williams, who refuses to read any book, anywhere, anytime, passed up the chance to read this one and he now has a blooming shrub where he used to have hair.

It's pretty, and the birds like it, but it's kinda itchy.

A whole second grade class in Connecticut told their teacher they didn't want to read this book, and now each kid is fruit-shaped.

Billy, the banana in the second row, wishes he could be a pineapple.

No one knows exactly why turning down this book has such a powerful effect on people.

But it never fails.

Avoid this book and you'll face certain trouble.

Ask Vincent . . .

Or Jessica . . .

Or Danny . . .

They all wish they'd read this book.

The good, good, good, good news is nothing that happened to any of them will happen to you.

Your head won't fall off. And you won't grow strange or unusual body parts.

You are 1,000,000,000% safe.

Because you have been smart enough to read this book.

Just be sure you read the *whole* book.

To the very last word . . . on the very last page.

Because nothing bad can happen to you if you read all the way through the whole book

Seriously.

THE END . . . FOR NOW

ANDREW ANSWERS

The whole thing started in Mrs. Wilson's class . . .

"Andrew, can you tell the class a word that starts with N?"

"No."

"Andrew, I want you to tell us a word that starts with N."

"Never."

"Andrew, I am asking you for a word that starts with N."

"Nope."

"Andrew, think. There are so many words that start with N, and you only have to name one."

"Nonsense."

"Andrew, you know the letter N. So, if I ask you, 'Can you name a word that starts with N?' what is your answer?"

"Nothing."

"Andrew, if you don't name a word that starts with N, I am going to have to send you to the principal's office. What do you say about that?"

"Nasty."

So, Mrs. Wilson sent Andrew to see Miss Fox, the principal. Miss Fox was kind, and she tried to give Andrew another chance.

"Andrew, maybe you don't like the letter N. So, let's try a different one," she smiled. "Can you tell me a word that begins with W?"

"Why?"

"Andrew, take a deep breath and tell me a word that begins with W."

"When?"

"Right now, young man. A word that begins with W."

"What?"

Now, as you already know, Miss Fox was kind. And she hardly ever got mad—except for that one time when Shelby Jordan painted all the erasers black instead of cleaning them. But anyway, Miss Fox tried again.

"Okay, Andrew, let's try another letter. Can you tell me a word that starts with L?"

"Later."

"Andrew, try again."

"Lunchtime."

"Andrew, tell me a word or I will call your parents. I want an L-word NOW!"

"Loser."

NO
NEGATIVE
NOPE?
NADA
NAH
NO
NO
NOPE
NO WAY
NO
N

That did it. Before long, Andrew's mom and dad were in the principal's office.

It didn't go much better there.

"I . . ."

"Impossible."

"T . . ."

"Tomorrow."

"R . . ."

"Ridiculous."

"C . . ."

"Can't."

"S . . ."

"Sorry."

"Y . . ."

"Yuck."

Before long, Andrew was sent to the school board.

"May we have a word that starts with A?"

"Absurd."

Andrew was sent to the mayor.

"Andrew, I'd like you to tell me a word that starts with G."

"Goodbye."

Andrew was sent to the governor.

"Andrew, let's end this foolishness. You can go right back to your classroom as soon as you tell me a word that starts with F."

"Foolishness."

So, Andrew was sent to the president.

"Andrew, I'm a busy person. But your teacher, principal, parents, school board, mayor, and governor all thought it would be a good idea for us to chat. I know they've all asked you to say words that start with particular letters of the alphabet. But here in the Oval Office, you can speak for yourself. Tell me what's on your mind, young man."

And Andrew said,

"**A**nybody
Big
Can
Do
Everything
For
Generally
Honest,
Intelligent,
Joking
Kids.
Listen,
Mighty
Nice
Office!
President
Questioning
Respectful
Student

Takes

Unbelievable

Vision.

Wahoo!

X-ray

Your

Zipper!"

The president thought for a moment, took a deep breath . . .

and awarded Andrew a full scholarship to the college of his choice. Starting that very day!

When asked why, the president said, "What else could I do? The kid's a genius!"

THE END

LEFT TO HIS OWN DEVICES

"Daddy," eight-year-old Ellen said. "Would you please drive me to Tracy's house?"

"One minute," her father said, barely looking up from his handheld device. "I just have to send this text."

Ellen sat down to read a book. She didn't mean to read the *whole* book while sitting there, but she had the time—because her dad didn't send *one* text, he sent, and received, dozens.

Ellen put the book down. She again asked: "Daddy, would you please drive me to Tracy's house?"

"One minute," her father said, barely looking up from his tablet. "I just have to download these files."

Ellen sat down to read another book. She didn't mean to read the *whole* book while sitting there, but she had the time—because her dad didn't download *one* file, he downloaded, and sent, dozens.

Ellen put the book down. She again asked: "Daddy, would you please drive me to Tracy's house?"

"One minute," her father said, barely looking up from his laptop. "I just have to send this email."

Ellen sat down to read another book. She didn't mean to read the *whole* book while

sitting there, but she had the time—because her dad didn't send *one* email, he sent dozens.

Ellen put the book down. She again asked: "Daddy, would you please drive me to Tracy's house?"

"One minute," her father said, barely looking up from his phone. "I just have to make a quick call."

Ellen sat down to read another book. She didn't mean to read the *whole* book while sitting there, but she had the time—because her dad didn't make *one* call, he made, and received, dozens.

And they *weren't* quick.

Ellen put the book down. She again asked: "Daddy, would you please drive me to Tracy's house?"

"One minute," her father said, barely looking up from his desktop. "I just have to order an item online."

Ellen sat down to read another book. She didn't mean to read the *whole* book while sitting there, but she had the time—because her dad didn't order *one* item, he ordered dozens.

While her dad was online, Ellen went outside (she had run out of books).

Sometime after, Ellen walked back into the house. Her dad smiled and said, "Okay, I'm finally all done. I'm ready to drive you to Tracy's house."

"Never mind," Ellen said. "I'm now twenty-three and I can drive myself."

THE END

Flute Schute

BECKY SCHMECKY

Becky was a lovely little girl.

But lately, her parents had noticed her acting, well, weird.

See, she had started rhyming. A lot. For no reason.

And her rhymes were kind of odd.

Like when she told her dad that she loved it when he played the "flute schmute."

And when she asked her mother for a new "hat schmat."

"Perhaps we should take her to the doctor," her dad said to her mom.

"Doctor, schmoctor!" replied Becky.

"Becky, dear . . . would you like to go to the mall?" her mom asked.

"Mall, schmall!" replied Becky.

"Let's go to the bank," dad said.

"Bank, schmank!" replied Becky.

"Let's go to the store," mom said.

"Store, schmore!" replied Becky.

"How about a trip to the library," dad offered.

"Library, schmibrary!" replied Becky.

"Let's go to the movies," mom said.

"Movies, schmovies!" replied Becky.

"Let's go to the park," dad said.

"Park, schmark!" replied Becky.

Dad didn't know what to do.

Mom didn't know what to do either.

"Do you want to go to the restaurant schmesterant?" she asked.

"Okay," replied Becky.

So, they did.

And Becky had a double helping of her favorite meal.

Chicken schmicken!

THE END (SCHMEND)

YOU CAN'T BE CEREAL!

Five-year-old Rex got up by himself. He made his bed by himself. He brushed his teeth by himself. He got dressed by himself. He poured a bowl of Munchy Flakes and milk by himself. He ate it with a spoon by himself. He wiped up all of the Munchiness he'd spilled by himself. He put away the box of Munchy Flakes and the carton of milk by himself. He washed his bowl and spoon by himself. And then, proud of his

accomplishments, he ran to his mom's room. Today was the big day!

"Mom, it's here! It's here! It's finally Take Your Child to Work Day!"

Mom looked at him and said, "Rex, uh, it's only two o'clock in the morning. I don't have to leave until eight."

Rex ran back to his room, got undressed, unruffled the blanket, hopped back into bed, and promptly fell asleep.

When Rex next opened his eyes, the sun was shining into his room. "Good morning, morning!" he exclaimed, unaware that his greeting made absolutely no sense. And then, Rex made his bed by himself. He brushed his teeth by himself. He got dressed by himself. He poured a bowl of Munchy Flakes and milk by himself. He ate it with a spoon by himself. He wiped up all the Munchiness he'd spilled by himself. He

put away the box of Munchy Flakes and the carton of milk by himself. He washed his bowl and spoon by himself. And then, proud of his accomplishments, he ran to his mom's room. Today was the big day!

"Mom, it's here! It's here! It's finally Take Your Child to Work Day!"

Mom looked at him and said, "Rex, uh, it's only five o'clock in the morning. I don't have to leave until eight."

Rex ran back to his room, got undressed, unruffled the blanket, hopped back into bed, and promptly fell asleep.

When Rex next opened his eyes, he looked at his clock. He happily saw it was 7:00 in the morning. "It's finally time!" he exclaimed. And then . . .

Rex made his bed by himself. He brushed his teeth by himself. He got dressed by himself. He

poured a bowl of Munchy Flakes and milk by himself. He ate it with a spoon by himself. He wiped up all the Munchiness he'd spilled by himself. He put away the box of Munchy Flakes and the carton of milk by himself. He washed his bowl and spoon by himself. And then, proud of his accomplishments, he ran to his mom's room. Today was the big day!

"Mom, it's here! It's here! It's finally Take Your Child to Work Day!"

Mom looked at him and said, "Okay, Rex, now it's time. I'll get ready and you go have breakfast."

"But mom . . ."

"No buts, young man! A bowl of Munchy Flakes and milk! March!"

Rex walked to the kitchen and poured himself a bowl of Munchy Flakes. He poured milk on it and slowly ate it all. He wiped up all the

Munchiness he'd spilled by himself. He put away the box of Munchy Flakes and the carton of milk by himself. He washed his bowl and spoon by himself. And then, his dad came into the kitchen and said . . .

"Good morning, champ. Today's the big day, huh? Goin' to work with mom! Fantastic!"

"Yeah, Dad, can't wait!" Rex said, even though he wasn't exactly sure where his mom worked or what she did.

"Sorry you can't ever come with me to work, son," Dad said. "But they have a strict 'no kids allowed in the sewer' law."

"I understand," Rex said.

"I know you'll have a blast in mom's office," Dad offered. "But first, a hearty breakfast," he added as he poured Rex a heaping bowl of cereal with milk.

"But Dad . . ."

"No buts, young man! A bowl of Munchy Flakes and milk! Perfect fuel for a busy workday!"

"Daaad . . ."

"Start eating!"

So, Rex did. He ate the whole bowl. And he drank the extra-tall glass of milk dad thrust his way.

Rex's mom came downstairs and grabbed Rex's hand to begin their big day.

Now, knowing that Rex had eaten so many bowls of cereal, you might be thinking that the kid threw up all over his mom's car on the way to work. Or you might be thinking he threw up all over his mom's desk at work. Or you might be thinking he threw up all over her boss as they shook hands.

But the truth is Rex didn't do any of those things.

What a relief, huh? Proud of Rex, huh? Not so fast.

When Rex and his mom got to work, Rex said, "I have a biiiiig tummy ache!"

His mom told him he was probably just excited, and it'd feel better once they settled in for the day's activities.

But Rex really didn't feel well. And when his mom's boss offered him a delightful bowl of Munchy Flakes, he yelled to her, "Munchy Flakes aren't delightful! In fact, I *hate* them!"

As it turned out, that wasn't the *best* thing to yell at the president of the Munchy Flakes Corporation, and Rex and his mom got sent home.

The following day, Rex's mom got up by herself. She made her bed by herself. She brushed her teeth by herself. She got dressed by herself. She poured a bowl of Munchy Flakes

and milk by herself. She ate it with a spoon by herself. She wiped up all of the Munchiness she'd spilled by herself. She put away the box of Munchy Flakes and the carton of milk by herself. She washed her bowl and spoon by herself. And then, proud of her accomplishments, she ran to her son's room. Today was the big day!

"Rex, it's here! It's here! It's finally Take Your Child Back to School Day!"

Rex looked at her and said, "Mom, uh, it's only two in the morning. I don't have to leave until eight . . ."

THE END

THIS LAND IS HIS LAND

"Sorry we missed your school concert, Matt," his mom said.

His dad continued, "Yeah, I had a meeting and Mom, well . . ."

"I'm afraid I misplaced my calendar and I forgot," Mom said.

"Sorry, Sport," added his dad.

"That's okay," Matt shrugged, even though things clearly weren't okay. After all, Derek's mom had postponed surgery and Reed's dad had

canceled a business trip so that *they* could be there. *Everyone's* parents showed up . . . except Matt's.

"I'd have given anything to hear you sing 'This Land is Your Land'" his dad said.

Well, now you never will! Matt thought to himself. Too bad!

"Hey, maybe you could give us a *private* concert," Mom said. But Matt pretended not to hear her as he ran up to his room.

That's when Matt had the idea. And he instantly knew it wasn't just a good idea. It was a *great* idea. The kind of idea that guaranteed, 100%, without a doubt his parents would never miss another performance.

"Maaaatt . . . what do you want for dinner?" Dad called from the kitchen.

Matt came halfway down the stairs and (to the tune of "This Land is Your Land") sang:

I'd like a salad
With fresh tomatoes
A piece of chicken
And mashed potatoes
Some chocolate pudding
A glass of so-o-da
That's what I want for dinner, please!

Dad smiled and started cooking as Matt went outside to shoot some hoops.

A little while later, it was dinnertime. Matt ate his food—exactly what he'd musically requested—without a word. And when he was finished, he sang (to the tune of "This Land is Your Land"):

Thanks for the dinner
It was delicious
Now I'll be happy
To do the dishes
Then please excuse me

I'll take a bi-i-ke ride
And promise to be home before dark!

Later that evening, as Matt lay on his bed reading, his mom and dad showed up at his door. He sang them an update . . .

I did my homework
I studied spelling
I took a bath so
Armpits not smelling
I'm pretty tired
I'll go to sle-ee-p soon
Goodnight, and kisses, Mom and Dad!

Mom snickered as she blew a kiss. Dad harrumphed a little but had a twinkle in his eye as they said goodnight.

The next morning, Matt bounded down, ate breakfast without a word, then sang . . .

I'll bring my football
It's show-and-tell day

I wish you both a
Terrific, swell day
I packed my lunch and
I hear the school-oo-l bus.
Enjoy your meetings, Mom and Dad!

Matt was quiet the whole ride to school. A few minutes after the bell rang at school, his teacher said, "Matt, please come up and do the first problem on the board." And Matt sang . . .

When doing math just
See what the sign is
Plus is addition
A dash is minus
You see this plus here?
That means to a-aa-d it
As we know, four plus four is eight!

Later, in gym, Matt sang . . .

I feel like doing
Something gymnastic

ARTISTIC JUICES FLOWING...

When I do back flips
I feel fantastic
Then let's play dodge ball
Or run some re-ee-lays
I love to get some exercise!

And in art . . .

Artistic juices
Are really flowing
Sculpting and drawing
Plus some Van Goghing
When I am finished
Call the muse-ee-ee-um
Art class is where I love to be!

Matt sang his way through his school day. And his teachers were amused. Mostly. Though they were all pretty glad it was Friday.

That whole weekend, pretty much the only thing anyone heard from Matt, they heard to the tune of "This Land is Your Land." Mom couldn't

stand it. Dad had surely had enough. But Matt kept it up, and back at school on Monday, when his teacher said, "Good morning," Matt responded . . .

Good morning, teacher
It's good to see you
We'll have a good week
I guarantee you
There'll be a class trip
And we'll be lear-rn-ing
Second grade is so interesting!

Eight or nine such songs followed that day, and by late afternoon, the teachers and principal had met to decide what to do about Matt's singing. Matt's parents were hardly surprised when they got a call that evening . . .

"Mr. and Mrs. Paris, this is Principal Nelson. It seems, well, it seems that your son Matt is, well, has been *singing* instead of talking ever

since the school concert. He isn't actually doing anything wrong, but it is, um, irritating the teachers . . ."

Matt's parents, who had been living with Matt day after tune-filled day, suddenly realized *why* the boy was singing. They told the principal that they had an idea how to get him to stop it.

That evening at dinner, Matt's parents knew what they had to do. They looked Matt in the eye and sang . . .

Please listen up, Matt
We're so regretful
We got too busy
Also, forgetful
We're very sorry
Yes, please forg-i-ive us
We'll never miss another show.

Matt thought for a minute, then smiled. And for the first time, he spoke. In words, not lyrics.

He said, "Thanks, Mom and Dad. I appreciate that."

And Mr. and Mrs. Paris never missed another of Matt's school performances.

THE END

IT MAKES SCENTS

"Attention, please. I'd like all of the third-grade classes to report to the auditorium at once," said the voice of the principal on the classroom PA system.

"Why do we have to go?" Brooke Newsom asked her teacher. It was the 17,203rd question Brooke had asked that day.

"I believe it's time for the school Smelling Bee," Mrs. Gittleman told her. "C'mon everyone, line up right now."

MAPLE STREET
ELEMENTARY SCHOOL

"*Smelling* Bee?" Brooke asked with a laugh. "You must mean *Spelling* Bee."

"No, *Smelling*," her teacher told her. "S-M-E-L-L-I-N-G."

"I know how to smell spelling," the girl said. "I mean, spell smelling."

"I'm proud of you," Mrs. Gittleman told her. "Now, let's go."

When the class reached the auditorium, they saw the big banner onstage.

"It *is* a Smelling Bee!" Brooke said.

"Welcome, everyone, welcome!" said Principal Gittleman, who was no relation to Brooke's teacher. (There were, in fact, seven people with the last name Gittleman working at the school; one principal, four teachers, the janitor, and the lunch lady—whose *first name* was Gittleman. It was a total coincidence, though, and none of them were related to each other.)

"Today, we are here to find out which student is the best smeller at Maple Street Elementary School. Smelling is important. After all, it is one of the five senses. Can anyone here name the other four?"

Michael Sykes, sitting in the front row, raised his hand. After Principal Gittleman called on him, he said, "The senses already have names."

Principal Gittleman smiled. "Yes, they do, Michael. Can you tell me what they are?"

"Taste, touch, hearing, and sight," he said. "And sometimes, Y."

"The senses are right," the principal told him. "But Y is a sometimes *vowel*."

"Oh, yeah," Michael said. "Do I win anyway?"

Principal Gittleman told him that she was sorry, but there was no prize for naming the senses. Then she told everyone how the competition worked:

"Two children from each class will be selected—at random—to come up and compete. You will each be blindfolded, and you will have to identify many different scents. Get one right, and you stay in for another round. But if you're wrong, you're out. The last contestant left wins the competition."

Principal Gittleman then showed off the trophy: a giant nose with the word MAPLE engraved on it.

Everyone *oohed.* A few people *aahed.*

"Mrs. Gittleman," Brooke asked her teacher. "Could you please pick me at random?"

"I'm sorry, dear," Mrs. Gittleman told her. "If I picked you, it wouldn't be at random."

Principal Gittleman then called up ten students—two from each class—by choosing a name at random from each of the five third-grade classroom lists.

When Jeffrey Fisher and Grace Williams were called to the stage to represent Brooke's class, Brooke pouted.

The ten students in the competition were each blindfolded, and then they took turns identifying various objects based on their smells.

Teddy Phillips correctly identified the scent of baby powder.

Amanda Gleason immediately knew the smell of shampoo.

Then Tiffany Douglas sniffed a sandwich that Mrs. Gittleman (the lunch lady) held up to her nose.

"Tuna from the cafeteria," Tiffany guessed. But she was wrong. It was meatloaf.

"Oh, yeah," Tiffany said. "It smelled just like tuna, so I should have known it was our school's meatloaf."

Mrs. Gittleman the lunch lady grunted. But Tiffany was out.

The competition continued until Marcus Jensen was stumped after taking a whiff of garlic (he guessed sweat socks), and Sara Day correctly identified the smell of a ripe banana.

"You, my dear, are the winner of the Maple Street Elementary School Smelling Bee!" Principal Gittleman told the girl. "You get the giant Maple Nose!"

Everyone cheered for Sara Day, especially after Principal Gittleman named it Sara Day. Everyone, that is, other than Brooke.

The other contestants left the stage quietly, except for Billy Rowe, who'd somehow forgotten to take off his blindfold and tumbled down the stairs.

With that, the assembly was over. The students and teachers all returned to their

classrooms, and for the rest of the afternoon, Brooke concentrated on one task. No, not smelling things; she was already good at that.

Rather, she practiced being selected at random.

"I'll get picked for the next Smelling Bee," she vowed. "Or my name isn't Brooke Gittleman!"

THE END

BOOK IT!

“We need someone to star in our new picture book,” said Helen, the very important editor at the Smashola Book Company.

With that in mind, she went on television and appealed to the public. “If you are very interesting, we might want to write a story about you. Come to 1270 Cottontail Street at 3:07 p.m. today.”

By 2:54, there was a line around the block. It seemed everyone in town wanted to be the star of a story.

Helen asked the first ten people to come to her office and line up.

One by one, they showed Helen why they thought they should be in a story.

Fritz Coyote played the violin with his toes, showing special symphonic skill.

"That song makes me sad!" Helen said. "Next!"

Chef Richard Snog juggled five coconut custard pies without spilling a crumb.

"Coconut gives me a rash!" Helen said. "Next!"

A sweet little girl dressed from head-to-toe in powder blue...

"*Powder blue*? I don't think so!" Helen said. "Next!"

Frieda the Magnificent Magician made fourteen doves appear out of her hat.

"Bird number twelve is a teensy-bit delightful," Helen said. "But as for the rest of the act . . . next!"

Stanley Hyenawitz told a 22-minute joke that Helen didn't understand at all.

Helen finally interrupted him and said, "Next!"

Helen called the next ten into her office.

"Next! Next! Next! Next! Next! Next! Next! Next! Next! Next!"

Then she called the next ten people in line.

"Next! Next! Next! Next! Next! Next! Next! Next! Next! Next!"

And then, just to save time, she went to the window with a megaphone and addressed everyone else who was waiting.

"NEXT!"

It seemed as if no one in town was interesting enough to be the subject of a Smashola Book Company story.

Helen sat alone for hours. And then, in the darkness, there was a tiny, tiny, tiny knock at the door.

When Helen answered it, a very tall woman with a miniature poodle rushed in. She quickly set up a stage full of mirrors, turned on a music player, and the poodle danced the most beautiful ballet anyone had ever danced.

Helen stared breathlessly at the stage throughout the performance.

And when the music finished, she didn't say, "Next!"

She didn't have to. Instead, she stood up and clapped her happiest clap.

"Hooray! Yippee! I've finally spotted a true star!" Helen cheered.

And indeed she had.

For while staring at the poodle's ballet performance in the mirrors, she was able to find a singular sensation—a very, very, very interesting subject for her story.

Helen clapped some more.

"I have found a very, very, very interesting subject for my story!" Helen beamed.

"Miniature poodle and her owner bowed in appreciation.

"Oh, you misunderstand," Helen told them. "I mean, that was a delightful dance by Miss Poodle. But *she* is not the star of my next book."

The pup looked at her quizzically. So did the owner. After all, the miniature poodle was the only candidate in the room.

Unless, that is, you count Helen herself.

Yes, while looking at the mirrors behind the poodle, Helen decided that the star of her next book would be . . .

Helen!

So self-satisfied, Helen laughed and giggled the rest of the day. She even chuckled herself to sleep, and then got up at 3 a.m. to laugh the jolliest laugh of all.

But this time she wasn't laughing with glee about her new book.

See, she *finally* understood the punch line of Stanley Hyenawitz's 22-minute joke.

It had been a good day (and night) for Helen. A very good day (and night) indeed.

THE END

DROP THE WHOLE THING

Millie's report for school, "A Day in the Life of My Family," was finally finished. It was 10:30 p.m. the night before it was due, and Millie was very tired as she stuffed the report into her backpack. The kid could hardly stay awake; but the important thing was her report was done.

Her parents weren't happy that Millie had stayed up so late on a school night. But they were proud that she had stuck with it, and they enjoyed hearing her read the report aloud.

The next day, Millie walked to school with her pals Randee and Aaron. It was a windy day. A very windy day. The kind of windy day that takes your hat and sweeps it clear across the courtyard. The kind of windy day that blows all the index cards out of your backpack as you're busy chasing your hat across the courtyard. And that's what happened to Millie . . . and to her report.

Randee and Aaron and Millie chased and grabbed and grabbed and chased and managed to catch every single card. The stack was sloppy, gloppy and way out of order, but at least Millie got to class with the whole report.

"I'll put it all back together during recess," she sighed. "No prob."

"Millie, you're first today," her teacher boomed. "Come up and read us your report."

Big prob.

"Um . . ."

"Is anything wrong?"

"Um, no."

"You *did* finish it, didn't you?"

"Um, yes."

"You *do* have it with you, don't you?"

"Um, yes . . ."

"Then please read it to us," her teacher insisted.

"Now?"

"*Now!*" her teacher bellowed. "I mean, yes, please. Now."

Millie got to her feet, slowly walked up to the front of the class. She began to read her report. It was waaaayyyy out of order . . .

The End.

47

I took a bath. I scrubbed. I rubbed. I used soap. I shampooed. And when I got out of the tub, I dried my body with

———

6

meat loaf, topped with mushroom gravy. Wow, there's nothing better.

———

14

I grabbed a large serving spoon and plopped a giant portion on my plate. Then I picked up my fork and ate every bite, because I figured that for dessert there'd be

———

16

muddy soccer cleats! Ooey, gooey, crusty dirt flicking and flying around.

———

2

I knew I'd better grab the vacuum and immediately suck up

______
3

Grandma's set of fake teeth!

______
9

What a big mistake! So of course I dropped it exactly where it belonged, in

______
10

the toilet.

______
31

My brother is two-and-a-half and it's about time he learned to

32

drive the minivan.

19

Dad came home early today, and asked me to help him wash the windows.

20

Mom walked by and put my brush and a tube of toothpaste in my hand. But when I looked down, I saw she had made a big mistake! This wasn't my ultra-double-bubble-fudge ripple toothpaste, it was the tube that was specially made to clean

______

8

my little brother's butt! It is always messy, and my parents expect me to dump his poop in

______

30

Dad's favorite slippers! How cute is that?

______

24

My brother Wally just came down the stairs, all by himself, taking baby steps in

23

cow manure for the lawn.

22

It was getting dark. Practice was over. I tiptoed into the house quietly so no one could see I was wearing

1

a towel that had a picture of a tiger on it.

7

Grandma came in and saw me! She welcomed me home and told me she'd been cooking all afternoon so she could serve me my favorite meal

---

12

all the dirt on the carpet.

4

Dad opened the hatchback and pulled out a giant bag. And he held his nose and said, "Whew, does this stink!" It was

---

21

Mom's wedding dress.

28

Since my birthday is coming up, I peeked in the closets looking for a present. I am really hoping for an awesome

______

25

pie á la mode.

______

17

But guess what I found hanging in the hall closet?

______

27

Uncle Sidney.

______

37

Mom came storming in, yelling, "You are so filthy! March right up to the bathroom and take a bath right now, young lady!"

5

My Uncle Sidney stayed for dinner. He's got a big appetite, and he just can't say no when the family is serving

---

13

poop in the potty.

33

I had homework to do. Uncle Sidney helped, and when it came to math, he knew

---

38

absolutely nothing.

15

Kitty walked by and I petted her fur. And then she dashed off, zipping around the room and

40

knitting a beautiful beret for

35

the cat across the street.

42

When we finished eating, Grandma decided to show off. She sat down and delighted the whole family by

______
34

hissing at

______
41

each of us and

______
36

then going pee-pee in

______
43

the litter box

44

a lot.

39

Dad started yawning. He'd had a long day, and since his sports car was being repaired, he was forced to

18

skateboard.

26

I hate having to spend so much time wiping the mush off

29

my pillow.

46

It had been a long night. So I kissed everyone goodnight, ran up the stairs, and rested my head on

45

the bathroom sink.

11

What Millie Meant to Read . . .

It was getting dark. Practice was over. I tiptoed into the house quietly so no one could see I was wearing

muddy soccer cleats! Ooey, gooey, crusty dirt flicking and flying around.

I knew I'd better grab the vacuum and immediately suck up

all the dirt on the carpet.

Mom came storming in, yelling, "You are so filthy! March right up to the bathroom and take a bath right now, young lady!"

I took a bath. I scrubbed. I rubbed. I used soap. I shampooed. And when I got out of the tub, I dried my body with

a towel that had a picture of a tiger on it.

Mom walked by and put my brush and a tube of toothpaste in my hand. But when I looked

down, I saw she had made a big mistake! This wasn't my ultra-double-bubble-fudge ripple toothpaste, it was the tube that was specially made to clean

Grandma's set of fake teeth!

What a big mistake! So of course I dropped it exactly where it belonged, in

the bathroom sink.

Grandma came in and saw me! She welcomed me home and told me she'd been cooking all afternoon so she could serve me my favorite meal.

My Uncle Sidney stayed for dinner. He's got a big appetite, and he just can't say no when the family is serving

meat loaf, topped with mushroom gravy. Wow, there's nothing better,

absolutely nothing.

I grabbed a large serving spoon and plopped a giant portion on my plate.

Then I picked up my fork and ate every bite, because I figured that for dessert there'd be

pie á la mode.

Dad started yawning. He'd had a long day, and since his sports car was being repaired, he was forced to

drive the minivan.

Dad came home early today and asked me to help him wash the windows.

Dad opened the hatchback and pulled out a giant bag. But first he held his nose and said, "Whew, does this stink!" It was

cow manure for the lawn.

My brother Wally just came down the stairs, all by himself, taking baby steps in

Dad's favorite slippers! How cute is that?

Since my birthday is coming up, I peeked in the closets looking for a present. I am really hoping for an awesome

skateboard.

But guess what I found hanging in the hall closet?

Mom's wedding dress.

I hate having to spend so much time wiping mush off

my little brother's butt! It is always messy, and my parents expect me to dump his poop in

the toilet.

My brother is two-and-a-half and it's about time he learned to

poop in the potty.

When we finished eating, Grandma decided to show off. She sat down and delighted the whole family by

knitting a beautiful beret for

each of us and

Uncle Sidney.

I had homework to do. Uncle Sidney helped, and when it came to math, he knew

a lot.

Kitty walked by and I petted her fur. And then she dashed off, zipping around the room and

hissing at

the cat across the street

then going pee-pee in

the litter box.

It had been a long night. So I kissed everyone goodnight, ran up the stairs, and rested my head on

my pillow.

THE END

SEE HERE!

Vanessa looked at the ad in the newspaper. It said:

Send only $14.99 check or money order plus $2.95 for shipping, $3.50 for handling and local sales tax, and $17.12 for no good reason and this very special pair of X-Ray Powered Binoculars will be yours! See through walls! See around corners! See down the block into the neighbor's house and know what they're having on their Munchy Flakes!

X-RAY
POWERED BINOCULARS
SEND ONLY $14.99
CHECK OR MONEY
ORDER PLEASE
$2.95 FOR SHIPPING
SEE THROUGH
WALLS!
X - RAY
BINOCULARS

"Oh man, this is too good to be true!" Vanessa exclaimed.

"Then it probably is," her mom said. "Those things never work."

"They *have to* work," Vanessa replied. "If they didn't work, they couldn't advertise them!"

Her mother snorted, then reminded her that ads and commercials always try to make products look better, taste better, or seem better than they really are. "That's what gets people to buy them, sweetie," Vanessa's mom chuckled.

Vanessa rolled her eyes, and said, "Well, I'm buying them anyway!"

Mom laughed her famous "that's what *you* think" laugh, and firmly told Vanessa that there wouldn't be any X-Ray Powered Binoculars in her future—because mom wouldn't be wasting more than $30 for them!

Vanessa then vowed to earn the money herself. And that's exactly what she did. She mowed lawns, she babysat, she sold lemonade, pretzels, and cookies. She fed dogs, she washed windows, and she wrapped packages at Mr. Horowitz's Nifty Gift Shop and Pizza Palace.

And pretty soon, she had a huge mess of coins that totaled up to $38.56!

Vanessa gave her mom the right amount of coins, and mom sent a check to order the X-Ray Powered Binoculars.

Every day the following week, Vanessa sat by the mailbox waiting for the mail carrier to bring her dream binoculars. And every day . . . nothing.

Same thing the following week. And the following week. And the week after that.

Finally, just as Vanessa had pretty much given up hope, the binoculars arrived. Vanessa ripped

open the package and found . . . a little tiny pair of plastic binoculars. They were so tiny, in fact, that Vanessa could make a fist around them and you wouldn't be able to tell they were even in her hand.

When her mom saw the itsy-bitsy binoculars, she couldn't help but laugh. She gave Vanessa a stern, 20-minute lecture about believing false advertising, wasting money, and so on.

Vanessa wanted to cry. But she didn't. She remained quiet during the whole lecture, and waited as mom left the room.

Then she aimed the binoculars at the living room wall and saw through that, through the garage next door, through the neighbor's house, around the corner, down the block and into her best friend Jenny's bedroom, where she spotted a bag of jelly beans she'd left there a few weeks ago.

"Mom's right—these are *junk*!" Vanessa said, tossing the binoculars aside and running out the door to go claim her long-lost jelly beans.

THE END

THE BID, BID MISTAKE

"Welcome to the great national book auction here in Washington, D.C.," the auctioneer said. "Please try to stay calm, as we auction off original works by some of the world's greatest poets to raise money to benefit the Foundation of Artists of Resourceful Thinking. Or, as the organization is more commonly known, F.A.R.T."

What followed was a four-hour auction unlike anything the literary world had ever witnessed. Collectors bid thousands of dollars on works

by noted poets such as Emily Dickinson, W.B. Yeats, and Walt Whitman. Some even bid on artifacts said to have been *owned* by famous poets, such as a tissue once used by Edgar Allan Poe and some leftover frosting from the desk of Robert Frost.

But it was the final book of the day that had the bidders leaping out of their seats.

That book—the only known copy of a work by Roberta M. Mahogany—was the much-sought-after, never-before-read book called . . .

Poetry by Furniture

Indeed, Ms. Mahogany had lived with furniture her whole life, and as her final poetic work, had interviewed various pieces around her home and put their thoughts into words.

Some said she was brilliant.

Some said she was a genius.

Others said she was nutty as a fruitcake.

But the crowd *oooed* and *aaahed* as the auctioneer held up the book and announced that bidding would start at one million dollars.

No one bid.

It wasn't that the people in the crowd weren't ready to spend a million dollars or more on the book. It was simply that no one had ever heard any of the poems.

"No one has ever heard any of the poems!" a disgruntled woman yelled from the third row. She wanted to hear a sample poem before spending such a large sum of money.

"Very well," the auctioneer said.

He opened the treasured book, cleared his throat, and read the first poem in the book to the hushed crowd.

"This is called 'The Couch.'"

I can vouch
It's nice to be a couch.
It feels great to help
people
be comfy
and cushy.
But please, please,
please
be good to me—
Dig deep down
and get the remote
control
out of my tushy.

"Simply breathtaking!" cried the woman in the third row.

"I must have that book!" yelled the man next to her.

"Read another epic poem, please!" called a man through tears of joy.

"Very well," said the auctioneer, knowing that the more the bidders heard the poetry, the higher they'd be likely to bid.

"This is called 'The Chair.'"

I look nice
in your living space.
But I won't ask you
twice . . .
move your butt, you're
sitting on my face!

The woman in the third row fainted at the magnificence of the poem. The man sitting next to her revived her, (though for a moment, he considered letting her stay unconscious so that she wouldn't outbid him).

"I will read one last poem before we start the bidding," the auctioneer told the throng. "This one is called 'The Ottoman.'"

F.A.R.T.

Though I'm a footstool
as comfy as a
fur-lined moccasin
it takes strength to be
an ottoman
And so, I take a daily
vitamin.

"Absolutely beautiful," the auctioneer said. "In fact, never mind one million dollars. I am starting the bidding at *two* million dollars!"

"I bid two million dollars!" a voice called from the back.

"Two million and a penny!" another voice shouted.

"Two million, seventeen dollars and twenty-three cents!" a third voice said.

"Two million, one-hundred-ninety-seven dollars . . . and a half of a jelly donut!" a fourth voice called.

The bidding went on and on, ultimately reaching five million dollars.

The auctioneer was about to accept that final offer, when someone who hadn't been heard from yelled, "One hundred million dollars!"

The crowd gasped.

The auctioneer accepted the one hundred million-dollar bid and brought the winning bidder to the stage.

"Congratulations on winning this precious Roberta M. Moahogany book," he said. "May I ask your name?"

The woman spoke softly. She said, "My name is Roberta M. Mahogany."

"You bought your own book?" the incredulous auctioneer wanted to know.

"Yes, I did."

"Do you *have* one hundred million dollars?" he asked her.

"No, but I will be earning that much from this sale," she told him.

"No, you won't," he said. "You have to pay that much to *receive* that much."

Roberta M. Mahogany thought about that.

"Oh. Um, I guess you're right," she said. "I withdraw my bid."

"You *can't* withdraw your bid!" the auctioneer fumed. "You made a firm bid, and I intend to hold you to it."

"But . . . but I don't have one hundred million dollars!" Roberta M. Mahogany said, starting to cry. She feared she would never smile again.

"I have one hundred million dollars!" yelled the woman from the third row. "It's right here in my purse. I will pay for the book and return it to its rightful owner—you!"

"Thank you," said Roberta M. Mahogany, hugging the woman. "Who are you?"

"My name is Helen. I am a publisher—and an author too. Perhaps you've seen the very famous book about me—the one that earned me fifteen billion dollars.

Yes, it was *that* Helen. She generously gave the one hundred million dollars to Roberta M. Mahogany, so that she could use it to buy her own book. After Roberta handed the money to the auctioneer, he gave it back to her, because, after all, she had written the book in the first place.

Roberta smiled. Then she laughed. A lot.

In fact, with the one hundred million dollars *and* her book in hand, she laughed all the way through the dinner meal she ate with Helen.

And she *especially* laughed when Helen told her Stanley Hyenawitz's joke.

THE END

BUY-BUY FOR NOW

"Kids, it's time for this year's fundraising effort," Mrs. Feinsilver told the class. "We are all going to work together to try to earn funds to pay for new playground equipment."

"Are we selling wrapping paper again?" Michael Williams wanted to know. "Because last year, my grandma said that she bought so much wrapping paper, she couldn't afford to buy any gifts to wrap!"

"No, not wrapping paper," Mrs. Feinsilver said. "It's . . ."

"I hope it's not candy," Jenna Douglas said. "The gooey chocolate always melts in my backpack when I'm delivering the orders, and people end up spending money for mush."

"Nope, not candy either," Mrs. Feinsilver told the girl. "This year, it's . . ."

"It had better not be seeds," Ralph Botner announced. "My mom said our garden is already full of plants that aren't growing."

"How can it be full of plants if they aren't growing?" Jenna asked him.

"I dunno," Ralph told her. "It's just what my mom says."

"*My* mom says we don't need any more kitchen gadgets." Jason Reiss said. "My big sister sold choppers and scoopers and peelers

and stuff, and none of it really worked. There's a whole drawer near our sink that's full of that junk, and we can't open it because the only thing we didn't buy was the stuck drawer opener-er."

"It's not kitchen gadgets," Mrs. Feinsilver reassured the boy. "Rather, we will be selling . . ."

"I know! It's probably gift cards good for local merchants!" Reilly McNeil guessed. "My cousin's school sold those, and we got a card redeemable for $25 worth of taffy. The school got $5, and I got . . . three cavities!"

"Not gift cards, Reilly," Mrs. Feinsilver said. "I'm glad to hear that you're all so enthusiastic and full of ideas, but we are actually going to sell . . .

"Magazines!" Eli Newsom offered. "Subscriptions to publications that nobody

wants, nobody needs, and nobody reads, as my father calls them."

"Well then, your father will be glad that we're not offering magazines," Mrs. Feinsilver said. "Now, I've been trying to tell you what we *are* selling . . . but you all keep guessing. So, I'll let everyone have a chance to guess before I reveal what it is."

Ideas flowed from all over the classroom.

"Buttons!"

"Mugs!"

"T-shirts!"

"Flowers!"

"Grand pianos!"

"Popcorn!"

"Live lobsters!"

"Lollipops!"

"Kitchen stools!"

"Toadstools!"

"Sore throats!"

"Zebras!"

"Okay, that's enough guessing!" Mrs. Feinsilver said. "What we are selling this year is . . . kindness!"

"Kindness?" Lily Harper repeated. "How do you *sell* kindness?"

"Well," Mrs. Feinsilver said, "we will all go around the neighborhood and do favors for people. Water their lawns. Walk their dogs. Things like that. And we will charge them each a small sum."

"But Mrs. Feinsilver," Eli Newsom said. "My dad says you're supposed to *give kindness away*."

"Right," Reilly McNeil added. "We should do those things out of the goodness of our hearts."

LIVE LOBSTERS!
LOLLIPOPS!
ZEBRAS!
BUTTONS!
SORE THROATS!
T-SHIRTS!

Every student in the class nodded in agreement.

"Well, that's very nice of you. And we can definitely do that. But . . . we will still need a fundraiser," Mrs. Feinsilver told them.

"How about selling wrapping paper?" Michael Williams suggested.

"Or candy," offered Jenna Douglas.

"Seeds! Let's sell seeds!" said Ralph Botner.

"Ooh, I know! Kitchen gadgets!" said Jason Reiss.

"People love gift cards," said Reilly McNeil.

"There's always magazines," Eli Newsom called out.

"Really, who cares what we sell?" Lily Harper said. "As long as we do it with kindness."

Mrs. Feinsilver smiled. Lily was right; it didn't really matter what the kids sold. The

teacher was just very glad to have a classroom full of kids who understand the importance of being kind.

And she wrote herself a note—to remind her to have a serious talk with Danny Watson, the boy who'd suggested that the class sell sore throats.

THE END

EATING HIS WORDS

"Mitchell, do you have a spelling test tomorrow?" Mrs. Marshall asked her son after dinner one night.

"Um, no. Maybe. I don't remember. I think so. Possibly. Perhaps," he replied.

"If you're not sure, then that tells me you haven't studied," his mother said.

"Uh, I remember now. The test isn't until Friday," Mitchell told her. "So I'm good."

"How good?" his mother asked. "This is Thursday night; do you know what that means?"

"Of course I do!" he said. "It means that my ninth favorite show is on!"

"No, it means you have to study your spelling words, because the test is *tomorrow*!" she informed him.

"Mom!" Mitchell whined. It was the kind of whine that said *no*, and *you're right*, and *help me*, all in the same non-word shriek.

"Hand me your spelling list, and I'll be glad to quiz you."

Mitchell grabbed his backpack and fished out a crumpled up, pudding-stained piece of paper that had obviously been in there since the alphabet had first been invented.

"Okay," Mrs. Marshall said, trying to de-crumple the page. "The first word on the spelling test is . . ."

"The first word is always our name," Mitchell said. "Mitchell. M-I-T-C-H-E-L-L. Mitchell."

"Very good," Mrs. Marshall said, fully aware that her son wouldn't get any points for knowing how to spell his own name.

"And the second word is Marshall. M-A-R-S-H-A-L-L."

"You're two for two," Mitchell's mother said. "Now let's try for the words that are actually on the list."

"Uh oh, now it gets harder!"

"The first word is general."

"Do you mean general as in an Army general? Or general as in non-specific?" Mitchell asked.

"They're spelled the same way," his mother informed him. "This is a list of homonyms."

Mitchell wasn't exactly sure what she meant by that. He was just glad she wasn't asking him to spell homonyms.

"Could you use the word in a sentence?" Mitchell asked. That was something he'd seen the contestants do in the National Spelling Bee on television.

"Of course. In general, the Army general felt very well."

"I see what you did there, Mom," Mitchell said. "Cool sentence."

"Thank you," Mrs. Marshall said.

"General. That's spelled J—"

"Nope."

"G . . ."

"Good."

"G-E-N-U—"

"There's no U."

"G-E-N-E-R-A-L. General."

"Very nice, Mitchell. Are you ready for the next word?"

"Y-E-S," Mitchell told her. "That spells yes."

"The word is second."

"Is that second as in the one after first, or second as in tick-tick on a clock?"

"Once again, they're spelled the same way," his mother informed him.

"Could you use the word in a sentence?" Mitchell asked.

Mrs. Marshall thought for a moment, before saying, "The boy came in second in the race; he only lost by one second."

"You're very good with those harmonies," Mitchell told her.

"Homonyms," she corrected. "Words that are spelled the same, and pronounced the same, but have different meanings. And thank you."

"Second," Mitchell said, writing the letters in the air with his finger. "S-E-C-O-N-D."

"Very nice," Mrs. Marshall said. "Next word is fethom."

"Huh? I've never heard that word before!" Mitchell protested.

"Gee, neither have I."

Mrs. Marshall took a closer look.

"Oh, wait . . . it's *fathom*. There was a clump of dried chocolate pudding covering up the 'a'."

"Oh."

"Before you ask, fathom can mean 'to understand.' It's also a linear unit of length—about six feet—to measure water depth."

"Gee, Mom," Mitchell said. "You're so smart."

"Thank you," his mother said, smiling. "But you still have to spell it."

"Want me to spell it? I-T. It. There. Done!" Mitchell said. "What's next?"

"Mitchell!"

"Could you use it in a sentence?"

"I can't fathom why there is chocolate pudding all over your spelling list," his mother said.

"By the way, did I tell you that you make the most delicious chocolate pudding in town? Maybe even the best in the state! You should open a chocolate pudding store: Mrs. Marshall's Marvelously Mouthwatering Pudding Palace," Mitchell said. "And not just chocolate! Other flavors too! You'd become a multi-multi-multi-multi-millionaire . . ."

"Stop stalling!" his mother replied. "The word was fathom."

"How do you spell that?"

"F-A . . . Mitchell! Stop it and start spelling!"

"Fathom. P-H . . ."

"No."

"F?"

"Yes."

"F-A-T-H-E . . ."

"Not E."

"U?"

"No."

"A?"

"No."

"I?"

"No."

"Y?"

"No."

"34?"

"That's a *number*, not a letter."

"Fathom. F-A-T-H. . . . I have a good idea."

"What's that, Mitchell?"

"You wait here, and I'll go ask my fathom how to spell it. Okay, mothom?"

"Not funny, kid. You named every vowel except one."

"I did?"

"Yes. Think about what you've learned in school. And if you can't remember vowels that way, think about what you've learned on *Wheel of Fortune*."

"Oh! O. Letter O. Fathom is F-A-T-H-O-M. Right, Mom? Right?"

"That's right. Good job."

Mitchell and his mother went over the whole spelling list. Mitchell was sure that he'd get all twenty words right. His mother was confident of that as well.

"And now," she said, "there's only one word left to discuss. Bedtime."

"Huh? That's not one of my words!" Mitchell protested.

"No, I mean it's actually your bedtime," his mother said.

"May I grab a snack before I go to bed?" Mitchell asked.

Mrs. Marshall was so glad he had said "May I?" instead of, "Can I?" She wasn't as thrilled that he'd said 'grab,' but that was a lesson for another time.

"Of course you can have a snack. Here's your spelling list," Mrs. Marshall said, handing the paper to her son.

"I know all of the words," he said. "Why do I need that?"

"It can be your snack!" she told him. "Just lick off all of the delicious chocolate pudding!"

THE END

GEG

THE GAME OF LIFE

"Come on down!" Wally Martin called from the kitchen table. "It's time to play . . . breakfast!"

Jenny and her little sister Molly stomped down the stairs and joined their dad at the table. They both enjoyed breakfast, of course, but they agreed it was a little unusual having a game show host for a dad.

See, everything he did, and everything he said, was like something you'd see on a game show.

"Welcome to *Win Your Breakfast*, Jenny," he said, sticking a breadstick in front of her mouth as if it were a microphone. "Please tell us where you're from and what you like to do."

"Um, dad, I'm from upstairs," she told him. "And I told you yesterday, I'm a fourth-grader and I like to play soccer."

"That's great, Jenny," Wally said. "And who'd you bring with you this morning?"

"I'm Molly," the little girl said. "I'm in third grade, and I like to tap dance."

"Please repeat that into the microphone, Molly," Wally said.

"Um, dad, it's a breadstick," she pointed out.

But Wally insisted, so Molly repeated—into the breadstick, "I'm Molly. I'm in third grade, and I like to tap dance."

"Hey there, Molly!" her dad said. "Okay, girls . . .are you ready for round one?"

"Maybe we could just *eat* instead of playing a game this morning," Mrs. Martin said. "Just for a change, like a regular family, I mean."

"Nonsense!" Wally said. "That would be boring. I made the breakfast, now it's time for the girls to win it!"

The girls and their mom sighed.

"Okay, girls, in round one, I'll show you some letters, and you have to unscramble them to name a breakfast food," Wally told them. "First one to get two right gets to choose this morning's jelly."

"Do we really have to?" mom asked.

"Yes! And here's your first word: G-E-G"

Jenny tapped her fork on the table—which was kind of the same thing as buzzing-in on a game show.

"Yes, Jenny?"

"Egg," Jenny said.

"That's right! You're the first person ever to *un*scramble an egg!" Wally said, injecting a small dose of game show humor.

"Okay, try to name *this* breakfast food," Wally said, holding up a card that read A-P-E-S-N-A-C-K.

Jenny again tapped her fork and said, "Pancakes."

"Ding! Ding! Ding!" Wally said. "You've won the round, and you get to select today's jelly flavor!"

"Grape," Jenny said.

"Okay, grape it is!" Wally said, cheerfully. "But don't be sad, Molly! You're behind, but you can still be a winner, 'cause it's time for the ketchup round!"

"Huh?" Molly asked.

"You can catch up, because it's the *ketchup* round!" Wally repeated. "Get it?"

"I guess so," Molly said, shrugging.

"Great! Here's how we play: I'll squeeze this container of ketchup onto my western omelet, and you have to name all of the ingredients before all of the ketchup runs out."

"Do I have to?" Molly asked.

"Isn't that a tremendous waste of ketchup?" Mrs. Martin asked.

"Not if she answers quickly," Wally told her.

Mrs. Martin smacked her forehead in disbelief.

"Okay, when I squeeze, start naming ingredients in this western omelet. Go!"

"Eggs, ham, mushrooms, onions, peppers . . ." Molly said.

"Ding! Ding! Ding!" Wally said, as he stopped squeezing ketchup. "That's exactly right, and the score is tied!"

"Way to go," Mrs. Martin told her daughter.

"Dad, can we eat?" Jenny wanted to know.

"In a moment, Jenny," Wally told her. "First, it's time for the bonus round. At the end of this round, one of you will win a ride to school in my brand new Maserati, a luxury vehicle appointed with silk and leather upholstery, heated front seats, a premium audio system, 19-inch aluminum wheels, adaptive air suspension, and more. It's a vehicle worth $76,780!"

"What about the girl who *doesn't* win?" Mrs. Martin asked.

"I'm sorry," Wally informed her. "The other contestant will ride in a 72-seat, bouncy, noisy yellow school bus that'll stop on every block between here and school."

"Wally!" Mrs. Martin shrieked. "You can't do that! Come on, girls . . . eat your breakfast, and *I'll* take you both to school on my way to work."

And that's just what happened.

As for Wally, he thanked the girls for playing, wished them a great day at school, and congratulated himself on getting out of having to drive the girls again. Then, as he did every morning, he went back to the bedroom, and greeted his bed as you'd expect a game show host would.

"Ah, my king-size memory foam mattress, with pressure-point relief, maximum spinal alignment, resistance to dust mites and allergens, supreme comfort and reliability, with a retail value of $2,649. It's time for the big snooze round! G'bye for now, folks, and thanks for playing *Win Your Breakfast!*"

THE END

THE SIGN
POSTED AT THE
ENTRANCE

A PORTION OF CAUTION

Christy thought the signs posted at the entrance made the whole experience seem pretty scary. It said:

"Extreme warning! You are about to enter a room where anything can happen. In fact, after you pass through this portal, it's likely that anything *will* happen. Get ready to explore regions you've never even considered.

Prepare to stretch your imagination like it's never been stretched before. You're about to face challenges unlike any you've ever known. Thoughts will soar through your head at lightning speed. You'll unquestionably encounter tests that will make you clench your fists, bite your nails, or possibly even scream out for help. There will be unexpected twists and turns. At times, you might feel sick to your stomach. There is no height requirement, but you are required to keep your wits about you and remain seated. You are urged to summon your inner strength at all times to combat these elements. Be brave. Be fierce. And remember, once you step inside, there is simply no turning back."

Christy had been to many haunted houses. She had ridden ferocious roller coasters in quite a few of the top theme parks. She was not a girl

who turned away from the unknown, no matter how fearsome it sounded.

And yet, for one brief moment, the one-percent "chicken" part of Christy told her to run. Run far in the opposite direction and get away while she still had the chance. She started to do that. But fortunately . . .

the other ninety-nine percent of Christy—the courageous part—told her not to run. It told her to turn back around, face the door, and enter with full control of her feelings and her head held high.

And that's just what Christy did.

She smiled a confident smile as she stepped inside.

"How bad could it be?" she said aloud as she shrugged. "*After all, it's only fourth grade.*"

THE END

WHAT DO YOU SNOW ABOUT THAT!

"This is a weather bulletin," the TV news reporter boomed. "There is a sudden storm, and we predict that three inches of snow will fall before midnight."

Mickey knew that a snowy evening forecast could mean there'd be no school tomorrow.

"But three inches is hardly enough to guarantee we'll have a snow day," Mickey said.

So he did what any snow-wishing kid would do. He took out his lucky coin, the one that his

grandpa had given him. According to Grandpa, the coin came with two lucky wishes in it.

Mickey had used one wish earlier in the year. He'd wished that his twisted ankle would heal in time for him to play in the baseball league championships. And it worked—his ankle was fine, and he played second base and batted cleanup. (The team lost 17-16 when Mickey struck out with the bases loaded in the final inning, but that wasn't really the coin's fault.)

Mickey believed that the coin held one more wish. So, following Grandpa's orders, he rubbed the coin three times with his right sleeve as he said the magic words . . .

"Coiny coin coin coin, do your stuff!"

Mickey turned back to the television screen.

"Here is a revised weather bulletin," the TV news reporter boomed. "That sudden storm that

we thought would bring us three inches of snow now looks as if it'll bring us three *feet.*"

"Whaaaat?" Mickey exclaimed.

"I said, here is a revised weather bulletin," the TV news reporter boomed. "That sudden storm that we thought would bring us three inches of snow now looks as if it'll bring us three *feet.*"

"Yippee!" Mickey shouted. "Thank you, news reporter! Thank you, magic coin! Thank you, grandpa!"

The TV news reporter continued, "Obviously, there won't be school tomorrow."

"I know!" Mickey shouted, doing a handstand on the couch.

"I know that you know!" the TV news reporter said. "And please don't do that on the couch!"

Mickey was too happy to even think about what the news reporter had said. The magic coin

had done its magical best, and there'd be no school tomorrow!

Suddenly, the news reporter was back on.

"Here is a revision of the revised weather bulletin," she said. "That sudden storm that we thought would bring us three feet of snow now looks as if it'll bring us . . . what? That can't be!"

"What?" Mickey asked. "What?"

" . . .snowmen! It is going to snow snowmen!" the TV news reporter blurted out.

"No!" Mickey said.

"Yes!" the news reporter answered. "Snowwomen too!"

Mickey knew that that was simply too much for the town to handle. He realized he'd wished too hard for snow. The magic coin had been *too magical*!

"I've got to undo the wish," Mickey said.

He reached for the coin, but unbeknownst to him, it had fallen out of his pocket when he was doing the handstand on the couch.

Mickey searched high and low for the coin. He covered every square inch of the room—except for between the couch cushions. (If you think about it, that's probably the *first* place to look for coins, but somehow, that didn't occur to Mickey.)

Mickey then ran to the window, thinking that perhaps he could wish on a star instead of the coin. But there weren't any stars in the sky. The only thing he saw was snowmen, hundreds of them, falling toward earth.

"Now I've done it!" Mickey exclaimed.

"Snowmen and snowwomen are falling from the sky!" the TV news reporter said. "This has never happened before, and no one knows what to do!"

But Mickey did. Being responsible for their arrival, Mickey somehow knew exactly what to do.

He put on his winter gear, walked outside, and greeted the snow people.

Suddenly a voice called out . . .

"Freeze!" a policeman yelled through a megaphone. "All you snow creatures—freeze!"

Um, they're already freezing, Mickey thought to himself. After all, they're made of snow.

Just then, more people from town arrived. Members of the rescue squad, firefighters, even the mayor showed up. They were all standing under a bridge, safely away from the snowmen.

"I think we should plow them!" a man said.

"Let's salt and shovel them!" another offered.

"No, let's melt them with ultra-heat ray guns!" suggested the mayor.

"Where do you get *those*?" someone asked.

"I don't know; I saw them in a movie once," the mayor said.

"Let's have a giant snowball fight with the snow people!" suggested the governor. "I haven't had a good snowball fight in years!"

"No one knows what to do!" the TV reporter said as she joined the group.

"I think I do," Mickey said, stepping out from the crowd.

"What?" the mayor asked. "Who said that?"

"I did," the boy said. "It's me, Mickey Valdez!"

"There is a boy among the very dangerous snow creatures," the news reporter said. "And no one knows what to do."

"They're *not* dangerous!" Mickey yelled. "And please stop saying no one knows what to do!"

"Plow them! Shovel them! Melt them!" the crowd started chanting. "Plow them! Shovel them! Melt them . . ."

"No! Let's *be kind* to them!" Mickey called back.

"How do we do that?" the governor demanded to know.

"Well, we could sing them a holiday song," Mickey said. He began . . .

"Deck the halls with boughs of holly . . ."

And the crowd chimed in, "Fa la la la la, la la la la!"

It was perhaps the loudest, most cheerful "Fa la la la la, la la la la!" ever sung.

And then . . .

The snow people started moving. Turning. Dancing.

So Mickey continued . . .

"Tis the season to be jolly . . ."

And the townsfolk added, "Fa la la la la, la la la la!"

And *they* began dancing too!

The singing and dancing continued for hours, and when they'd sung every holiday song they knew, everyone stopped, looked around, and saw that the snow people had built a truly spectacular snow village. It was a winter carnival unlike anything anyone had ever seen.

The joyous celebration continued for weeks. Until one day . . .

"This is a weather bulletin," the news reporter boomed. "It will be extremely warm today, and, I'm afraid our snow village will melt."

Everyone knew that it meant it was time to say goodbye to the snow people too.

"This has never happened before!" a different reporter said. "No one knows what to do!"

But once again, Mickey knew exactly what to do.

He went home and learned a lot more holiday songs . . .

and called his grandpa to ask for another magic coin, so that he could bring back the happy snow people another time.

(By the way, Mickey's school was open every single day that winter. After all, snow people don't cause traffic delays.)

THE END

IT ALL "ADS" UP

"I'm late for work," Frankie's mom moaned at exactly 7:59. "The school bus comes at 8:03, so you've got four minutes. Grab your bag, grab your lunch, and grab a seat in the minivan!"

"It's not polite to grab," Frankie's sister Molly pointed out from her high-chair. "Right, Mom?"

"Right, dear," Mom answered, even though she had no time to discuss manners. "Francis, let's go!"

Frankie (everyone called him that except his mom) grabbed one last handful of scrambled eggs.

"Maaaa, Frankie's eating eggs with his hands again!"

"Am not!"

"Oh, then why are your fingers yellow? And why's your fork so clean? Huh? Huh?"

"Mom, Dad, how come you let Little Miss Nursery School pick on me?"

But they didn't answer. Frankie's mom just took his hand to lead him to the minivan.

In a flash, Frankie's mom was busy zooming down their driveway to have him join the seven other kids who caught the bus on the corner of Fanton Hill and Easton Turnpike.

"See, we're early! No one's even here yet," Frankie pointed out.

"No, we're late! Everyone's already been picked up," his mother corrected. "Now I'll have to drive you to school, which will make me even more late for work!"

"I can write you a note," Frankie offered. "Maybe Mrs. Watkins will excuse you this time!"

Frankie's mom smiled (a little) as she started the two-mile drive to school, and she said, "Mrs. Watkins won't mind that I'm late. It's just that my client is expecting a new advertising slogan at our 2 p.m. meeting today, and I haven't come up with one yet."

"Well then, you shouldn't have watched TV last night, right, young lady? You know the rule: no TV until all work is done!"

"Funny, Francis," his mother interrupted. "But knock it off. Pernock's Peanut Butter is expecting a brilliant slogan by early this afternoon, and I'll have to—"

Now it was Frankie's turn to interrupt.

"Pernock's? I love that stuff! David's mother buys it! Cameron's mother buys it! But *you* never buy it!"

"I didn't know you like it."

"Like it?" Frankie asked. "Like it? I *love* it! It's goopy, it's gloppy, it's gooood!"

Frankie's mom slammed on the brakes and the car came to a sudden halt.

"Mom, what are you doing? We're still two blocks from the school!" Frankie asked.

Frankie's mom shouted, "Pernock's Peanut Butter: It's goopy, it's gloppy, it's gooood!"

"Yeah, that's what I just said!"

"Yes, my boy," his mom beamed. "And soon, all of America will be saying it! *That's* the new slogan!"

"It's amazing, just amazing," said Mrs. Jackie Watkins, president of the Watkins Advertising Agency. "Sales of Pernock's Peanut Butter have gone through the roof!"

"Well, it's better than sticking to the roof. Of your mouth. Get it? Peanut butter? It sticks to

the roof of your mou . . . never mind," said Ross Julian, the advertising agency's art director and occasional jokester.

"And Myra," continued Mrs. Watkins. "It's all because of your great slogan. All together now—it's goopy, it's gloppy, it's gooood!"

Clearly, the slogan had become a cheer throughout the office.

Mrs. Watkins then told Ross and Myra that because of their success with Pernock's, other companies were calling the agency to request new slogans and commercials.

"In fact," she said. "We have a meeting with Landman's Dairy at 10:00 a.m. tomorrow to try to help them advertise their butter. Myra, I hope you'll get plenty of rest so that your thinking cap will fit well in the morning."

That didn't really make total sense to Frankie's mom, but she knew what her boss

IT'S GOOPY
IT'S GLOOPY
It's
GOOD
PERNOCK'S PEANUT BUTTER

meant. So she promised to do her best, told the others goodnight, and went to her car for the trip home.

"Butter, butter, butter, butter . . ." Frankie's mom told herself as she drove. In fact, she was so deep in buttery thought, she drove right past the family's driveway. Twice.

As usual, the next morning was full of delays. For what seemed like the 4,532nd time this school year, Frankie and his mom missed the bus.

"This is a shame, Frankie," his mother said. "I could have been out of the house hours ago—I've been up since four in the morning, thinking about the campaign for Landman's Dairy."

"Landman's Dairy?"

Frankie's mom explained all about the new client she had to meet, and how they were looking for a new slogan for their butter. Right away, Frankie had an idea . . .

"How about—Landman's Butter: it's goopy, it's gloppy, it's gooood!"

"I don't think so," his mom told him. "That slogan was great for Pernock's. But it's already selling peanut butter; I can't use it for another product," she sighed.

Frankie shrugged. And he realized that sharing a slogan was probably like copying answers on a test. Not a good thing.

"Besides," his mother continued. "I've tasted Landman's butter. It's goopy. It's even gloppy. But it's *not* good."

Frankie couldn't believe what he was hearing.

"Well, if it's not good," he asked, "isn't it lying if you tell everyone to buy it?"

Frankie's mother explained that commercials try to make every product seem wonderful. "But that's not being dishonest. Let's face it," she

added. "*I* don't like Landman's, but other people might."

Frankie said he understood. He thought about all the toys that looked amazing in ads, and then were pretty crummy when he got his hands on them.

Frankie's mom laughed, and said, "Sometimes you have to say the wrong thing for the right reason. Or maybe it's the other way around."

Now Frankie was confused.

"It's like when you got that ugly sweater from Aunt Norma. If you'd said, 'Ugh, what an ugly sweater,' it would have hurt her feelings and she might have stopped giving you gifts.

"Wait," Frankie said. "By just saying, "thank you, I love it," I'm advertising for more gifts?

"In a way, yes," his mother said.

"But why am I advertising for more ugly sweaters?" Frankie wanted to know.

"Perhaps that's not a good example," his mom said. "The point is my agency gets paid to help companies sell their products. In this case, we have to do a commercial for butter and make it seem terrific."

Frankie got it. "And not just terrific," he snickered. "Butterrific!"

Frankie's mom slammed on the brakes and the car came to a sudden halt!

"Mom, what are you doing? We're still two blocks from the school!" Frankie asked.

Frankie's mom kissed him on the forehead, as she shouted, "Landman's . . . it's Butterrific!"

"Yeah, that's what I just said!"

"Yes, my boy," his mom beamed. "And soon, all of America will be saying it! *That's* the new slogan!"

A few weeks later, Mrs. Watkins found out that Frankie came up with the award-winning slogans. She hired him for $5,000,000 a year.

THE END

THE CANTDECIDES

On the north-west-southeast corner of Walk and Don't Walk is the beautiful red-pink-blue-green-orange-yellow home of the Cantdecide family.

The house is so many different colors because when they visit a paint store to pick a color, they *can't decide.*

They also can't decide what kind of furniture or decorations to have inside the house. What kind of pet to adopt. Where to go on vacation.

And they especially can't decide what to watch on television. If they invited you over, you'd likely see channels wildly flipping on the TV—though you wouldn't actually get to view a show. (You'd also see the remote being passed around the room; they can't even decide who gets to control the television.)

They are a family of four who simply can't decide anything. Nothing. Nada.

"Mom, mommy, ma, mother," the littlest Cantdecide said to his mother one morning. "Would you make me some breakfast? I mean, dinner. Lunch. Brunch. Snack. Breakfast."

"Yes. No. Yes. No. Yes," his mother told Vincent, whose name was Walter the day before. "What would you like?"

"Pancakes. Corn flakes. Wait, waffles. Um, eggs."

Not waiting for her son to change his mind again, the boy's mother begin to crack some eggs.

"Would you like *two* eggs, dear?" she asked.

"One. Seven. Three-hundred-and-twelve. Two."

She cracked two eggs, and asked the boy how he wanted them cooked.

"Scrambled. Fried. Baked. Omelet-style. Oh, hard-boiled."

"I already cracked them dear, so they can't be hard-boiled."

"What can't be hard-boiled?" the boy's sister asked as she bounded halfway down the stairs, then slid down the bannister the rest of the way. (Her name was Albany that morning; she's picking a different state capital every day. Or every week. Perhaps every month.)

"Your brother's eggs," their mom told her. "And my, don't you look lovely in that tank top, sweater, poncho, pants, skirt, dress, and overcoat!"

"Thank you," the girl squealed. "I put this on because I'm meeting Barbara at the beach. Or

I might go horseback riding with Ella at the tennis courts. Perhaps I'll spend some time fishing with Mike inside the new downtown department store instead."

"Sounds terrific," her mom said. "Also awful, horrible, and wonderful."

The morning went on like this. The boy never actually got his two eggs because his mother decided to use them to make muffins, which turned out to be croissants. And the girl ended up going miniature golfing with a baseball bat inside a darkened movie theater (at last count, her score on a par 3 was 712).

It is time for me to end this story. And I plan to end it happily. Or maybe it'll be a sad ending. It's hard to say.

Why? Because I am the father of the Cantdecide family. And frankly, when it comes to finishing this story, I simply can't decide.

I'm very sorry. No, I'm not. Yes, I am. Nope. Yep.

You'd better turn the page.

No, don't.

Yes, turn the page.

No, wait.

It's up to you.

Good choice!

I wish I could be more decisive.

No, I don't.

Yes, I do.

THE END (OR MAYBE NOT)

REGGIE CAN'T COME ALONG

"We're leaving for vacation in a few minutes," Dad said early one morning. "And I probably should have told you sooner, but Reggie can't come along."

"What?" the boy wanted to know. "What?!?!?"

"I'm sorry, it's just not possible."

"But . . ."

"Listen sport, getting to the airport would be too hard."

"I can't believe this."

"And think about the hotel."

"Daaaaaaaad!"

"There'd be quite a scene when we go to nice restaurants."

"Come on! Pleeeeeease!"

"Then there's the rental car to consider."

"Yeah but, yeah but, yeah but . . .!"

"Sorry, it's just the way it is. And the way it is, is the way it is."

"Does mom know about this?"

"Yes, it was her idea in the first place."

"Waaaaaaaaaaaaaaaaaaaaaaaaaaaaaaaaaaaa!"

"There's no use crying. The decision has been made and it's final."

"But dad, but dad, but dad, but dad, but dad, *but dad* . . ."

"Relax, it's just a two-week trip and then you'll be able to snuggle with your friend all you want."

"I won't be able to sleep the whole two weeks! *Not a wink*!"

"Oh, son!"

"It's not fair! It's not fair! It's not, not, not, not fair!"

"Okay, it's time to start the trip. Say goodbye to Reggie! See you later, Reggie! So long, Reggie! We're off!"

SLAM!

"Waaaaaaaaaaaaaaaaaaaaaaaaaaaaaaaaaaaaaaaaaaaaa!"

"This is going to be an absolutely marvelous trip!!"

"I'm *so glad* we left Reggie home!"

"The trip would have been terrible if we'd brought him!"

THE END

REGGIE'S
ROOM

MR. OG

The substitute teacher entered the classroom and greeted the class.

"Hello, everyone, my name is Mr. Ogimunkallowestangickumookillomastongopunawugelleedish.

How do you say that?

Well, it starts with OG as in HOG."

"Please try it."

The class said, "OG."

"Good. Then it's IM as in SWIM."

I AM
MR. OGIMUNK
ALLOW

"Say that, won't you?"

The class said, "IM."

"Good."

"Now put them together."

"OG-IM."

"Great. Then it's UNK as in SKUNK."

"Add the UNK. Now you've got . . ."

The class said, "OG-IM-UNK."

"Moving on," the teacher said. "Next add ALL as in BALL. Okay?"

"So it's . . ."

The class said, "OG-IM-UNK-ALL."

"Exactly. Now add OW as in COW."

The class said, "OG-IM-UNK-ALL-OW."

"Super! Let's add EST as in NEST. What have you got?"

The class said, "OG-IM-UNK-ALL-OW-EST."

"Well said," the teacher told them. "Now, ANG as in CLANG."

The class said, "OG-IM-UNK-ALL-OW-EST-ANG."

"You're doing great. Try it a few times, please."

The class said, "OG-IM-UNK-ALL-OW-EST-ANG!
OG-IM-UNK-ALL-OW-EST-ANG!
OG-IM-UNK-ALL-OW-EST-ANG!"

"Nice! Ready to add ICK as in TRICK?"

The class said, "OG-IM-UNK-ALL-OW-EST-ANG-ICK."

"Yes! We need to add UM as in GUM!"

The class said, "OG-IM-UNK-ALL-OW-EST-ANG-ICK-UM."

"Good. Next, OOK as in BOOK."

The class said, "OG-IM-UNK-ALL-OW-EST-ANG-ICK-UM-OOK."

"Hooray! Can you say ILL as in DRILL?" the teacher asked them. "Of course you can."

The class said, "OG-IM-UNK-ALL-OW-EST-ANG-ICK-UM-OOK-ILL."

"Say it again, please."

The class said, "OG-IM-UNK-ALL-OW-EST-ANG-ICK-UM-OOK-ILL."

"I love this class. Now, it's OM as in good old MOM."

The class said, "OG-IM-UNK-ALL-OW-EST-ANG-ICK-UM-OOK-ILL-OM."

"Bravo. It's time for AST as in CAST."

The class said, "OG-IM-UNK-ALL-OW-EST-ANG-ICK-UM-OOK-ILL-OM-AST."

"Way to go! To finish, here's an easy one . . . ONG as in STRONG."

The class said, "OG-IM-UNK-ALL-OW-EST-ANG-ICK-UM-OOK-ILL-OM-AST-ONG."

Repeat three times, please. Louder!

The class said, "OG-IM-UNK-ALL-OW-EST-ANG-ICK-UM-OOK-ILL-OM-AST-ONG!

OG-IM-UNK-ALL-OW-EST-ANG-ICK-UM-OOK-ILL-OM-AST-ONG!"

"Catchy, isn't it?"

"Listen carefully . . . OP as in MOP!"

The class said, "OG-IM-UNK-ALL-OW-EST-ANG-ICK-UM-OOK-ILL-OM-AST-ONG-OP."

"Know what comes next? UN as in BUN."

"That's not hard to say. And please pass the mustard."

The class said, "OG-IM-UNK-ALL-OW-EST-ANG-ICK-UM-OOK-ILL-OM-AST-ONG-OP-UN."

"Awesome! That's followed by AW as in SEESAW!"

The class said, "OG-IM-UNK-ALL-OW-EST-ANG-ICK-UM-OOK-ILL-OM-AST-ONG-OP-UN-AW."

"Marvelous! Can you do two at a time? How about UG as in BUG and ELL as in SMELL?"

The class said, "OG-IM-UNK-ALL-OW-EST-ANG-ICK-UM-OOK-ILL-OM-AST-ONG-OP-UN-AW-UG-ELL."

"Ahhhhhhh to the bug! But you're terrific! Okay, we're almost there! Let's add EED as in SEED and ISH as in FISH."

The class said, “OG-IM-UNK-ALL-OW-EST-ANG-ICK-UM-OOK-ILL-OM-AST-ONG-OP-UN-AW-UG-ELL-EED-ISH.”

“Awesome! I’m Mr. OG-IM-UNK-ALL-OW-EST-ANG-ICK-UM-OOK-ILL-OM-AST-ONG-OP-UN-AW-UG-ELL-EED-ISH-OCK-AB-ED-AT-ACK-EN-GO! Say that three times fast, won’t you?”

The class said, “Mr. OG-IM-UNK-ALL-OW-EST-ANG-ICK-UM-OOK-ILL-OM-AST-ONG-OP-UN-AW-UG-ELL-EED-ISH-OCK-AB-ED-AT-ACK-EN-GO!

Mr. OG-IM-UNK-ALL-OW-EST-ANG-ICK-UM-OOK-ILL-OM-AST-ONG-OP-UN-AW-UG-ELL-EED-ISH-OCK-AB-ED-AT-ACK-EN-GO!

Mr. OG-IM-UNK-ALL-OW-EST-ANG-ICK-UM-OOK-ILL-OM-AST-ONG-OP-UN-AW-UG-ELL-EED-ISH-OCK-AB-ED-AT-ACK-EN-GO!”

“Fantastic!” the teacher told the class. But . . . you can call me Bob!”

THE END

A SORRY STATE OF AFFAIRS

Dear Mrs. Cummiskey,

I am writing this note to say that I'm sorry I yelled out the answer in class. I was just so excited by the question, my answer somehow zipped from my brain to my mouth, and burst out through my voice before I had the chance to remind myself, *Mrs. Cummiskey doesn't like it when we yell out answers.*

I'm also sorry that the answer I yelled out was wrong. When you asked us to name the

sixth president of the United States, I *knew* who it was (I'm really good at naming all of the presidents in order, except for Millard Fillmore, whom I always forget but somehow just remembered). So, I really did know the answer, but I had been thinking about snack time, and that's why I yelled out, "John Quincy Pretzels."

And please forgive me for sticking out my tongue at Lisa Harper when she laughed at me and said, "Who was his vice president, John C. Potato Chips?" In truth, it was John C. Calhoun, so Lisa was showing that she knew her presidential history, so I should have smiled and complimented her. But somehow my reaction zipped from my brain to my mouth, and my tongue burst out toward Lisa before I had the chance to remind myself, *Mrs. Cummiskey doesn't like it when we stick out our tongues at other people.*

By the way, you are an excellent teacher. And I'm not just saying that to get out of trouble. I have learned more this year than I learned in all of my other years of school. I wish you could be my teacher forever, but of course, I know that can't be. I'm pretty sure you're only good with third-grade knowledge, and that teaching fourth or fifth grade would be too hard for you.

Thank you for understanding my calling out, and please know that I appreciate it that you didn't send a note home to my parents, like you did the time that I wrote my report on the making of mirrors with all of the words backward—so that you had to *read it* in a mirror. I thought it was funny and clever. You didn't. Neither did my mom or dad.

So please don't ban me from Field Day or the pizza party or any of the other fun stuff that's planned for the rest of the year.

Thank you.

Your student,

Kevin

PS: Also thanks for not telling my parents when I used all of your sticky notes to spell out HI TEACHER on your desk.

THE END

THE STUPID MESSAGE AT THE END OF THE BOOK

Okay, you've read this book until the end.

Will your head fall off?

We are going to let the head of our publishing company determine that.

His name is Leonard Cantdecide. And here's what he says . . .

"Yes, no, yes,

no, yes, no . . ."

You'd better close the book and walk away while your head is still attached. Goodbye.